THE COOKIE
Yes....
No....
Maybe...
I ALWAYS GET WHAT I WANT
MANNY SHOWALTER & DAYLON SHOWALTER
I0742094

Author's Note: *The Cookie* was written to help instill values in children and young ladies, to teach them how to respect not only themselves but their bodies as well, and to truly let them know that they are more than just another piece of cookie!

Proceeds from this book will be donated to the Sandra Showalter Williams
Youth Foundation (www.sswyf.org).

Disclaimer

The information provided in this book is designed to provide helpful information on the mature subjects discussed. This book is not meant to be used, nor should it be used to influence an individual's decision. The subject matter of this book should be discussed with an adult or guardian. The publisher and authors are not responsible for and are not liable for any damages or negative consequences from any decision, treatment, action, or results to any persons reading or following the information in this book.

This is a work of fiction. Names, characters, businesses, places, events, and incidents are either the products of the author's imagination or used in a fictitious manner. Any resemblance to actual persons, living or dead, or actual events is purely coincidental.

Creator

Manny Showalter

Authors

Manny Showalter

Daylon Showalter

Creative Director

Pria Showalter

Illustrator

Paul Goldman

E-mail: paul.goldman@customwebguru.com

Production Company

Mandaylan Productions

The Cookie

Manny Showalter and Daylon Showalter

It's the end of the day at Showalter Middle School. Robbie spots Lauren at the locker, and decides to ask Lauren for some of her cookie. Robbie approaches Lauren at the lockers.

"I love cookies. Can I please have some of your cookie," he says eagerly.

"I would let you have some, but my mother told me I can't share my cookie," she replies timidly.

"But I only want a little bit, a tiny piece, Lauren, that's all," he pleads.

Later on that day, Lauren meets up at the park with Ashley, a spunky, sweet brown-skinned girl, with a look of mild confusion.

Ashley shouts to her in an overly excited tone, "Hey, Lauren, what's up, girl!"

Lauren takes a moment to sort her thoughts. "Nothing much. Well, Robbie just asked me for some of my cookie."

Ashley shoots over to Lauren, hiding her curiosity. "So? All the boys do. Did he like it?"

Lauren hesitates. "Well, I didn't give him any. My mom and dad said I wasn't supposed to."

"Why? It won't hurt anybody if you gave him a little piece," Ashley says.

Little Lauren gets home to find her parents in the living room watching TV. A strong, earnest father is coupled by a loving, nurturing wife.

"Hey, Mom, hey, Dad!" Lauren shouts.

"Hey, baby girl," her dad replies.

"How was school?" her mom asks.

"School was fine, but I have a question." The room's energy changes as they sense the lightheartedness leave the room.

Alex, her dad, curiously replies, "Go ahead, I'm all ears."

"Well, why can't I share my cookie?" she questions.

Alex has a look of impending discomfort on his face while Kelly tries to camouflage her surprise. The TV is now off, and both parents are facing Lauren.

Alex wipes his brow and chokes down a nervous gulp. "What would make you ask that, Lauren?"

Lauren recollects the events of her day leading up to this question.

"I was in school, at my locker, and Robbie asked if he could have a piece. I didn't give him any, but why shouldn't I share? Ashley told me it's no big deal."

Her mother interjects, "Well, dear, you can't share your cookie with just anyone because it is valuable, and it's yours. If anyone can have a piece of the cookie, you won't have any left for someone special who deserves it."

"Also, sometimes these boys try and see just how many cookies they can have in the jar at once," her father adds, with a look of reflective horror.

Kelly and Alex are still sitting side by side in the living room, at the bottom. Above is their wedding day photo illustrating them in the midst of saying their vows.

Kelly recounts the details of her and Alex's younger days. "Well, I knew Alex was the man I wanted to share my cookies with when we got married."

Alex's smile conveys his genuine admiration of his wife. "And guess what, baby girl?" he asks.

Lauren asks, "What?"

"She saved that cookie and waited, but it was worth it because I learned to love and respect her for her and not for her cookie," he concludes.

Her parents are looking down. Lauren has a calm, pensive look about her.

"So what age did you get married?" Lauren eagerly exclaims as if waiting for the ending to her mother's fairy tale.

"I was twenty-three, and your father was twenty-five," Kelly responds.

"Oh, okay, you guys are trippin', trippin'! On that note, I'm gonna go to my room, thanks," Lauren says.

"You are very welcome. You can always talk to us."

"Your father's right. We love you, Lauren," Kelly reassures her.

"I love you guys too, thanks," Lauren says as they all embrace.

The next day, all the children are at the park. Lauren and her friends are beside the basketball court, hanging out, chatting and watching the boys.

"There goes your boy, Lauren," Ashley says in a teasing tone.

"No way! Your boy? Who, which one?" Violet shrieks.

Ashley lowers her tone, looking around suspiciously as if to spot an eavesdropper. "Oh, you didn't know, girl? Robbie's got his eye on Lauren, asked for some of her cookie yesterday and everything."

Violet gasps, almost appalled. "Whoa, you guys, my mom said we shouldn't share yet."

Lauren hears Violet, interested that her mom's word matches that of her own mother's. "That's not my boy, Violet, and you know what? My mom said the same thing."

"Girl, please, our parents just tell us that 'cause they don't want us having any fun of our own!" Ashley snaps.

"So you didn't give him any yet?" Violet whispers, eyes wide with surprise.

Robbie and the gang are shooting around before they start another game. Suddenly they all come to a halt as Robbie stops dribbling to look at the group of girls.

Bryce steals the ball out of Robbie's hands. "Jeez, Robbie, at least pass me the ball before you start drooling over them," he mocks.

"Shhhhh, look look look," Robbie rebuts, still staring.

"So what's the big deal?" Bryce shrugs.

Robbie leans closer to Mark and Bryce. "The big deal is, I asked Lauren for some of her cookie yesterday."

"So what? I got some of Ashley's cookie and Stacy's," Mark says in a very matter-of-fact manner.

Robbie replies with a proud air about him, "Yeah, but Lauren still has all her cookie."

It's the first day back from spring break Lauren stares out the window in homeroom, a gloomy, despondent look on her face.

Ashley approaches gleefully, and with a high-pitched whine, she utters, "Heeeeeeey, Lauren!"

"Hey," says a sad, pouty Lauren.

"What's wrong with you, girl?" Ashley replies, kind of consoling.

Lauren takes a deep breath, trying to summon the courage to say all the things she has been thinking. "I think I made a huge mistake, look." Lauren shows Ashley her cookie locket with what seems to be a piece missing. "I gave Robbie some of my cookie a few days ago, and we haven't spoken since."

"Giiiiiirl, oh no, you didn't!" Ashley shrieks in a loud whisper. "Did he like it? What happened to not sharing? You gonna keep hanging out with him?" Ashley replies, on the edge of her seat to hear the tea.

Lauren's eyes grow wide. "Shhhhh! Be quiet! I don't know, he was just so nice to me and made me feel special. I shouldn't have done it," she says in a hushed tone, way quieter than Ashley's.

"Okay okay, don't be a baby about it. It's not a big deal, Lauren," Ashley explains.

"It may not be for you, but it is for me!" Lauren snaps angrily through gritted teeth.

"What's that supposed to mean?" Ashley exclaims.

"Nothing." Lauren gets up, grabs her things, and leaves.

Lauren is walking to her locker when she sees a group of girls snickering. Continuing down the hall, she sees a group of girls eye her with disdain. The weird energy broadcasted from the other students unnerves Lauren slightly.

Lauren asks, "Hey, Roxy, what is up with everybody today?"

Roxy's eyes get wide as she turns to face Lauren. "Well . . .," Roxy pauses to sort her words.

"Well, what?" Lauren wonders intently.

"Well, everybody knows about—"

Before she can respond, Lauren interjects, "About what?"

"You and Robbie!" she blurts as if the sentence she was holding back in her mouth was hot coal.

Lauren's jaw drops, and she begins to pace. "Wait until I see him!" Lauren snaps back. "I can't believe he would do this to me."

Lauren is hunting the halls for Robbie, asking anyone and everyone if they've seen him. She spots him and darts toward him, snatching him by the arm away from his conversation with Bryce into a private section of the hallway around the corner. Robbie's face is puzzled and a little afraid. Lauren can hardly get her words out; she's so frustrated.

Lauren asks, "Why! Why, Robbie?"

"Why what? Lauren, calm down," he says, puzzled.

"Don't tell me to calm down. I trusted you! I shared with you when almost everyone told me I shouldn't have!" Lauren says in a stentorian tone.

"Lauren, I don't know what you're talking about. Just tell me what's going on!"

She pauses, unable to fully explain how she feels. Her face begins to turn red, and her eyes well a little bit. Still silent, Robbie breaks the stalemate.

"Later, Lauren, you're making me late for gym." Robbie leaves, annoyed and confused.

Distraught, Lauren turns and speeds away, barely able to contain herself, when she spots Amanda, Ashley, and Roxy on the way to the gymnasium.

Ashley asks, "Hey, girl, wassup?"

"Robbie told everyone I gave him some of my cookie! And when I asked him about it, he had the nerve to play dumb!" she says, barely able to maintain her normal, tranquil demeanor everyone has grown so used to.

The girls grow silent, desperately avoiding eye contact.

Robby comes into the boys' locker room.

"Wassup, fellas?" he yells into the muggy, crowded locker room. His friends chime in and begin gathering around him almost instinctively, as if they could tell by his mischievous grin he has news of something much more interesting than usual.

"Man, where were you yesterday? We were short a man at the park and had to pick up skinny Lenny."

Robbie chuckles hard, barely able to regain his composure before proudly boasting, "I was with Lauren. We were at my house."

Mark rolls his eyes. "Ditching us for Lauren again? Not cool, bro."

Robbie's eyes cut, and he lets out a mischievous chuckle.

"No way, you didn't!" says Bryce.

"Oh, but I did!" exclaims Robbie.

A brief silence comes over their section of the locker room, as if the world halted.

Then the locker room erupts with celebration, and Robbie embellishes his tale of conquest more and more with each detail, feeding off the crowd of boys pining for answers and explanation.

"It was simple. All I did was hang out with her a couple times, and she couldn't wait to share. I was over her house Saturday."

"Oh, you mean when you ditched us and didn't come to Bryce's house?" Mark says.

Robbie replies, "That's not the important part, Mark, but yes, that time, that's when she gave me some of her cookie."

Mark whispers to Bryce, "Pay up."

Bryce reluctantly pulls out a crumpled five-dollar bill from his pocket and hands it to him.

"Does that mean you're gonna start hanging out with us again?" The boys all laugh.

Lauren walks late into the gymnasium. The gym is packed and full of children eyeballing Lauren, and there is a strange energy in the room. She runs up to her clique—Roxy, Ashley, and Amanda—to see that they are displaying the same standoffish energy.

Lauren says, "Hey, girls, how is it goin'?"

They all create a task to do with the main goal of avoiding Lauren's gaze. Lauren is taken aback by the way her friends are treating her, especially in one of the times she needs them the most. She walks away from the girls, defeated and mildly confused. When the gym teacher begins to take roll, Mr. Costa, a tall, gruff mountain of a man, approaches Lauren after reading all the names before him.

Mr. Costa asks, "Lauren, why are you late, and why aren't you dressed out for class?"

Lauren stammers and stutters nervously.

Mr. Costa replies, "Well, 'um . . . um . . . ah-ah o-o-ohhh' isn't an answer. Half credit today, Lauren."

Lauren can't take it anymore. She quickly rushes out of the gym, on the brink of sobbing.

Mr. Costa scratches his head, puzzled. *What'd I do?* he wonders to himself.

Lauren's inner monologue as she races down the hall is, *I know he told everyone, he had to. My life is over. My friends don't want anything to do with me. What am I gonna do? Who knows, who doesn't know?*

Lauren is sobbing in the bathroom when she hears a disembodied voice say, "It's not *that* bad in here."

A nerdy short girl with Coke-bottle glasses, freckles, and a matted nest of hair comes out of the stall, with her science textbook. "You're that Lauren girl. Why are you in here crying? You're popular," she says in a puzzled tone.

Lauren continues to sob.

"Oh, jeez, don't cry, don't cry." Annalise begins playing peekaboo, her face even more contorted every time she removes her hands to reveal it. Lauren begins to smile, and then before she's aware, she erupts with laughter.

"What are you doing?" Lauren replies, barely catching her wind from the laughter.

"I don't know. It works with my little brother."

"Well, thanks . . . I needed that," Lauren replies.

"Wanna tell me what's wrong, or is it none of my business?"

Lauren pauses and then thinks for a minute and begins to tell her story. "I shared my cookie with this boy I really liked, and he hasn't spoken to me since, not to mention my whole gym class knows now on top of anyone else he told, and to make everything worse, my friends won't even talk to me."

"Is that all? I don't even have friends or have a guy I like to share my cookie with!" Annalise lets out a loud, obnoxious laugh concluded by a snort. "But seriously, that boy doesn't matter. Neither does the other girls and boys. Do you like yourself, Lauren?"

Lauren pauses briefly to digest the question. "Y-yes . . . I do."

"Well, what does it matter what they think? If I was half as pretty as you, I know I wouldn't. My mom tells me all this stuff doesn't matter anyway."

Lauren comes home from school. Annalise's wise words had slowly worn off with every look and hushed whisper she received in the hallways and on the bus. Her book bag is dragging against the ground. The minute she walks through the door, both her parents recognize her gloomy demeanor.

Alex gets up to greet her. "Hey, baby girl, is everything okay?" he says in a nurturing but probing tone.

Lauren hesitates, squeaking out a barely audible no. Kelly can tell by Lauren's response that her daughter is hurting. She rushes over toward Lauren and Alex. They both ask what's wrong many times before a tear rolls down her face, and Lauren finally explains all that occurred.

"I didn't listen to you guys, and I made a huge fool of myself. Everyone at school looks at me like a mutant now, and the boy I like won't even talk to me."

She starts getting more and more emotionally frustrated.

"Boy you like?" Alex has a contorted, forced look of compassion on his face, masking his paternal horror.

"What didn't you listen to us about?" Kelly interjects, focusing on the important topic.

There is a long pause of silence, followed by admission. "Well, I've been hanging out with Robbie a lot the past few weeks, and I felt like I really liked him . . . and he really liked me, so I kinda . . . kinda shared my cookie with him."

"You did what, young lady?" Alex scolds. "Go to your room, you're grounded!"

Lauren is devastated, crying in her room. What she had thought to be a minor error has made it feel as though her whole teenage life is falling apart. The handle of her door wobbles, and her heart races like never before. It is her father, but instead of the frustration and distress he had displayed downstairs, it is all but washed away, replaced by genuine care and concern for his beautiful young daughter. He walks up to her and hugs her silently for a while. His lips part suddenly, and in a sharp tone, he utters, "I apologize for how I reacted." As if almost embarrassed by his lack of composure, he says, "I love you and your mother loves you. We always will, and nothing will ever stop that, so you can always talk to us."

The tension in Lauren's body leaves, her mind relaxing to listen and not defend.

"We just want to make sure you make the best decisions. So we would prefer if you heeded our advice, but I understand you're a teenage girl, and you want to live and experience things. But some mistakes are very painful and very avoidable," Alex continues.

Kelly comes into the room and sits on the other side of Lauren. "Your father's right. We only want you to be happy, but we also have to protect you."

"Protect me from what?" asks Lauren.

Alex clears his throat. "Well, among other things, boys. Remember when I told you some boys just wanna see how many cookies they can have at one time? Well, they don't always play fair, nor do they always respect and appreciate a young lady for more than that."

Kelly smiles at Lauren and Alex, admiring her man's navigation of the situation.

"You're gonna be okay. You're strong like your father."

"And smart and beautiful like your mother," adds Alex.

Kelly adds, "When a man actually cares for you, your cookie isn't really on his mind. He's interested in you and figuring out why you're so special to him, and he'll want to make you feel as special as you are to him. Worry about yourself for now, and one day you'll find a man who can't help but feel special about you and just wants to make you happy, not for your cookie or anything else, but because he cares about you."

"Your mother is right, baby girl, especially the worry-about-yourself part."

They all laugh in a picturesque embrace.

Lauren has gone through most of the school day successfully, even hanging out with her newfound friend Annalise. She's getting ready to head to math class when she sees Robbie. All the anxiety she thought her parents had alleviated came back as she sees his arms around Amanda. Amanda, her own friend, is walking with the only boy she had ever had feelings for. Her face drains of color, becoming a pale hue of her golden skin that people are accustomed to.

She grits her teeth and feels an ambush of everything—anger, fear, betrayal, sadness—but through the oppressive feelings, a spark of hope ignites inside of her. She embraces this newfound fact and realizes that Amanda has taken a huge problem off her at last. His brash, callous disregard for her feelings has broken his spell on her. With her mind clear and rationally reflecting on not only her parents' but also Annalise's strong words of encouragement, a small tear flows down her face and around the corner of her lip, where a confident smirk has emerged.

To Be Continued . . .

MOOD
BY A MILLENNIAL

MOOD
BY A MILLENNIAL
MOOD
BY A MILLENNIAL

We hope you enjoy this book and receive the message. Our goal is not to generalize all young men as being like Robbie in the story. We understand that not all boys behave in the same manner. Our main focus is to protect young girls from being preyed upon. We want to emphasize that this is not about one race of girls being more promiscuous than another. This book is written for young ladies to understand the importance of pregnancy prevention and to make it easier for parents, guardians, and administrators to have the "birds and the bees" talk. Each of the girls in the story could be any young girl, as they are all being taken advantage of in some way by a young man. Our message is for everyone, regardless of race or age, and we aim to keep it clear and concise. It is not our intention to portray one race of young girls as being more promiscuous than others. All young girls are at risk of being taken advantage of.

-*The Sandra Showalter Williams Foundation*

This is to all of the young ladies who are trying to navigate through life as you strive to be the best version of yourselves. Be sure to focus on your strengths and strengthen your weaknesses. Self-respect is essential! People tend to treat you the way that you treat yourself. You are a prized possession, so never allow just anyone access to your body, your heart or your mind. Your reputation precedes you-always think before you act! You are very special and should always be treated as such. I sincerely hope that your future is bright and filled with people worthy of you!

-Felicia Showalter

"It's not about how you start. It's how you finish. We all have insecurities, but it's how we choose to overcome them that will set us apart from the rest. A girl who knows what she's working with is capable of having the world. It's yours for the taking whenever you're ready. LOVE YOURSELF instead of loving the Idea of people loving you. Settling is the lowest of the lows, the bottom. You are worth more than that despite your flaws, failures, or limitations! Before anyone else can be moved by who you are, you have to see it first with your own eyes. You have to be the one who sees your potential. You have to be the one to see your beauty. You have to be the one to see your power, whether it be a strong, boisterous force or a calm and stealthy current. You have to believe you are deserving of love. Be patient with yourself. Be understanding."

-Pria Showalter

To all the young ladies out there coming into their own and confronting situations that they have never encountered before, or even situations you're just uncomfortable with, I want to remind you that you determine your worth and no one else. Do what you want to do and love yourself for doing it. Those that are worthy to be around you will celebrate your happiness with you. Anyone trying to coerce, force or manipulate you is simply a grain of sand on your path to peace. It's important to keep your head up and your vision clear. Walk the path you desire because often times as young adults (male or female) we make decisions based on the opinions of those around us. Pleasing those around you is by no means bad, but make sure that you make decisions that satisfy you. Life can only be lived forward and understood backwards. If there's some wisdom I could impart to those younger than me, it would be to do what feels right to you! There is no right or wrong way, only your way and the ways others choose. You are powerful and valuable. Your voice is valid, so when you here that little voice in your head guiding you, it may take you exactly where you want to be.

-Daylon Showalter

Self-value is something crucial that young ladies ought to possess. Self-Value provides one with morals, and the knowledge to recognize how they are a living individual and not one's puppet that can be manipulated. Respect symbolizes confidence, individuality, and admiration of one's self.

-Hunter Atterbury

To every young lady who needs to know just how valuable you are, you are special in every way. Despite any past mistakes you may have made while not being aware of your worth, you are worthy. You can move forward starting afresh knowing that you deserve respect. A female's reputation is one of the most important qualities that she possesses. The more exclusive you are the better...as merit is placed on being "hard to get." It is important to carry yourself in a way that commands respect. Never forget...you are the prize!

-Manny Showalter

About the Authors

Manny Showalter has a bachelor's degree in business. He is an author, entrepreneur, as well as a motivational speaker. He has developed a program for teenagers and young adults that will teach them about financial literacy, paying for college, addictions and bad habits, teenage pregnancies, among many other things Manny Showalter is passionate about reaching the youth. He is the founder of Sandra Showalter Williams Foundation (sswyf.org), the inventor of protect your egg-head protection for sports and the owner of Mandaylan Production, which writes television and movie treatments for the entertainment industry.

Daylon Showalter is currently attending college studying psychology and is an actor-model and writer, represented by one of the top talent agencies in Atlanta, GA. Daylon currently sits on the board of Sandra Showalter Williams Foundation. Also he has directed the web series Girl Talk Bistro.

Follow us On Our Social Media Platforms

@thecookiechildrenbook
@showalterfoundation
@manny_showalter

The Cookie
Showalter Foundation
Manny Showalter

Check out our websites at
www.moodbymillennial.com

If you would like to partner with us and make 20-50% net profits selling our wonderful books, go to
www.helpthechildren.net

The Cookie

HOW CAN WE PRESENT THE IDEA OF ABSTINENCE TO OUR DAUGHTERS TO MAKE THEM EVEN CONSIDER GIVING IT A GO? THIS IS WHERE THE COOKIE COMES INTO PLAY! PARENTS, GUARDIANS AND TEACHERS THIS IS AN AWESOME ICEBREAKER TO SEGUE INTO THE BIG TALK. THE COOKIE WAS WRITTEN FOR GIRLS WHO HAVE THE INCREDIBLY DIFFICULT DECISION OF UPHOLDING TRADITIONAL BELIEFS AND VALUE SYSTEMS THAT HAVE BEEN PASSED DOWN BY OLDER GENERATIONS IN THE NEW ERA OF BEING PROMISCUOUS AND EXPERIMENTING AT AN EARLY AGE. IN AN IDEAL WORLD, GIRLS WOULD REMAIN VIRGINS UNTIL THEY ARE MATURE ENOUGH TO HANDLE ALL THAT COMES ALONG WITH MAKING SUCH A LIFE-CHANGING DECISION. NEEDLESS TO SAY, THIS IS FAR-FETCHED IN THIS DAY AND TIME. NO MATTER THE PATH YOUR CHILDREN CHOOSE FOR THEMSELVES, READING THE STORY OF LAUREN AND ROBBIE IS A GREAT WAY TO COMMUNICATE, LEARN, AND DEVELOP INTO AN ADOLESCENT IN A FUN WAY!

100% OF THE NET PROFITS WILL BE DONATED TO CHARITY

MANNY SHOWALTER &
DAYLON SHOWALTER